# YOU'RE THE
# APPLE
# MY

Written ...ny Rudner

Illustrated by Peggy Trabalka

ISBN 0-9642206-0-1


Printed and published in the United States by
Windword Press. Publisher is in Farmington Hills, MI 48334.
1-800-718-5888

Library of Congress Catalog Card Number: 94-90321

No tree was sacrificed to print this book.

To every child everywhere
no matter who you are

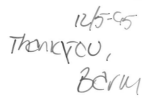

To Kit,

Thank you for sharing yourself with me.

Love,

Nancy Welday

December 1995

Of all the ways
I wish to say
that you are
just the best,
I haven't found
the words just yet
that truly pass
the test.

I haven't even
found a way
to show you
how I'm feeling,

like walking
on the air
we breathe,

or dancing on
the ceiling.

3

I could carve
your face
upon a rock,

4

a heart
upon a tree,

then add
the letters
of our names,
the names of
you and me.

I could pull
the petals
from a bloom
and wonder,
"yea or nay",

or find a date
that isn't used
to be your
holiday.

7

I'd sail across
the seven seas
to find a
number eight,

8

or wrestle with
the arms
belonging
to the hands
of fate.

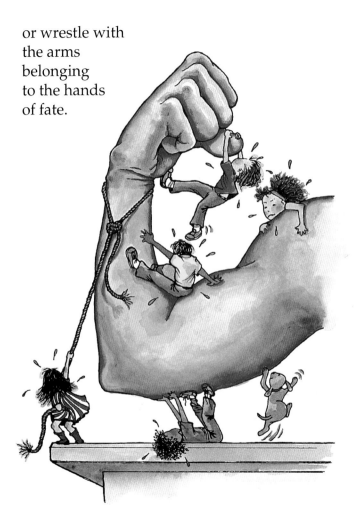

I'd try to tell the whole wide world there's more than seven wonders.

I'd dance
for rain
even though
it scares me
when it thunders.

I'd cook a soup
with you in mind,
it's called,
cream of the crop.

12

I'd quest to find
the highest peak
with your flag
at the top.

13

You'd be the prize
that I would find
within a
cereal box.

Within a meadow
you would be
the flower
of the flocks.

15

You're better than
a double scoop
of ice cream
after dinner.

16

You could finish last
in any race
and always
be the winner.

You have
more worth
than all the gold
within a
buried treasure.

You weigh upon
my mind so much,
the largest scale
can't measure.

You'd be
the puddle
in the rain
that somehow
I can't miss,

the joy
of angels
in the snow
upon the
frozen bliss.

21

You're one
in any million
if it had
just one
more zero.

You'd be
the cape
and mask
I'd wear
to feel like
a hero.

23

I'd sound
the trumpet
just for you
if I could blow
a note.

24

In all parades
yours would be
the first
and grandest
float.

If I had wings
you'd be
the lift
that I
would need
to fly.

If I could
paint the
clouds above,
your face
would fill
the sky.

27

You're out of this world,

the cat's meow,

divine,

the salt of the earth,

the cheese,

the peach,

the pick of the bunch,

beyond what
money's worth.

Just so you
will not forget
you're all
that I embrace,
the best
was saved
for last,
for you're
the apple
of my face.

**About the Author...**
Barry Rudner lives in Keego Harbor, MI
basking in the wind, the water,
and the word.

**About the Illustrator...**
Peggy Trabalka has lived, worked
and illustrated in Milford, MI
for more than thirty years.

**About the Publisher...**
Windword Press would like you to take two of
these before bed and call us in the morning.
You can tell us how you feel at
1-800-718-5888.